ABOUT THE AUTHOR

MIKE WAS BORN AND RAISED IN ST.HELENS, MERSEYSIDE. ALONGSIDE PLAYING SPORT AND BOARD GAMES, HIS FIRST INTERESTS INCLUDED ILLUSTRATING - SKETCHING HIS FAVOURITE CHARACTERS AND CREATING NEW ONES. MIKE LATER STUDIED MATHEMATICS AT DURHAM UNIVERSITY, WHERE HE MET HIS FUTURE WIFE, EMMA. AFTER A SHORT SPELL WORKING AS AN ACTUARY, MIKE TRANSITIONED INTO RECRUITMENT BEFORE BECOMING AN HR MANAGER FOR THE LONDON 2012 OLYMPIC AND PARALYMPIC GAMES. THIS CAREER PATH LED TO 4 YEARS IN BRAZIL, WORKING FOR THE RIO 2016 GAMES, WHERE HIS SON, JACOB, WAS BORN. THIS WAS FOLLOWED BY A YEAR IN TURKMENISTAN, WHERE MIKE WAS CHALLENGED BY HIS WIFE TO WRITE AND ILLUSTRATE A BOOK FOR JACOB; HENCE THE PUMPOSAURUS WAS BORN! FOLLOWING SOME CONSULTING WORK IN LIMA, PERU, MIKE RETURNED TO THE UK FOR THE BIRTH OF HIS DAUGHTER, MADELEINE. HE NOW LIVES IN CAMBRIDGESHIRE, WHERE HE HEADS UP THE GLOBAL HR TEAM FOR A SCIENCE AND TECHNOLOGY CONSULTING BUSINESS.

To/ Jack,

Happy Pumping!
From.
THE PUMPOSAURUS
& Mike

MIKE PAINTER

THE PUMPOSAURUS

OLYMPIA PUBLISHERS
LONDON

WWW.OLYMPIAPUBLISHERS.COM
OLYMPIA PAPERBACK EDITION

A CIP CATALOGUE RECORD FOR THIS TITLE IS
AVAILABLE FROM THE BRITISH LIBRARY.

ISBN: 978-1-78830-153-4

THIS IS A WORK OF FICTION.
NAMES, CHARACTERS, PLACES AND INCIDENTS ORIGINATE FROM THE WRITER'S IMAGINATION. ANY
RESEMBLANCE TO ACTUAL PERSONS, LIVING OR DEAD, IS PURELY COINCIDENTAL.

FIRST PUBLISHED IN 2018

OLYMPIA PUBLISHERS
60 CANNON STREET
LONDON
EC4N 6NP

PRINTED IN GREAT BRITAIN

DEDICATION

THIS BOOK IS DEDICATED
TO MY DAUGHTER, SON AND WIFE.
TO MADELEINE, JACOB AND EMMA
WHO, TOGETHER, MAKE MY LIFE.

YOU MAKE MY WORLD A BETTER PLACE,
WITH GIGGLES AND WITH FUN.
YOU'RE A LOVELY WIFE-OSAURUS,
GORGEOUS DAUGHTER AND GREAT SON!

THERE WAS ONCE A LITTLE DINOSAUR,
IN A LAND QUITE FAR FROM HERE,
WHO HAD A LITTLE PROBLEM WITH
EXPLOSIONS FROM HIS REAR...

HE LOVED TO PLAY OUT WITH HIS FRIENDS,
IN PUDDLES THEY WOULD JUMP,
BUT EVERY TIME HE PLAYED WITH THEM
HE COULDN'T HELP BUT PUMP!

HIS MUMMY AND HIS DADDY
BOUGHT HIM SHINY PURPLE WELLIES.
THEY SAID IT DIDN'T MATTER
THAT HIS BOTTOM BURPED OUT SMELLIES...

THEY BATHED HIM AND THEY PICKED OUT
ALL HIS BELLY BUTTON FLUFF,
BUT HE'D MAKE EXTRA BUBBLES
WHEN HE COULDN'T HOLD A GUFF!

HIS FRIENDS LOVED PLAYING FOOTBALL
AND HE LOVED TO JOIN IN TOO.
A KICK-ABOUT WITH EVERYONE
WAS WHAT HE LOVED TO DO...

THE PROBLEM WAS THAT SOMETIMES
HIS FRIENDS WOULD NEED A PEG,
FOR SOMETIMES WHEN HE BOTTOM-BURPED
IT SMELLED LIKE ROTTEN EGG!

THEY ALSO PLAYED LOTS IN THE PARK,
A PLACE OF SUCH FUN THINGS,
WITH ROUNDABOUTS AND CLIMBING FRAMES,
WITH SEESAWS AND WITH SWINGS...

THE PROBLEM WAS THAT SOMETIMES
HIS FRIENDS WOULD COUGH AND CHOKE.
FOR SOMETIMES WHEN HE BOTTOM-BURPED
IT CAUSED A FOGGY SMOKE!

THEY ALSO LOVED A PICNIC,
WITH SANDWICHES THEY'D MAKE.
THEY'D ALL BRING CRISPS, FRESH FRUIT AND SALAD,
FIZZY POP AND CAKE...

THE PROBLEM WAS THAT SOMETIMES
HIS FRIENDS HID BEHIND THE ROCKS,
FOR SOMETIMES WHEN HE BOTTOM-BURPED
IT TASTED OF OLD SOCKS!

THEY LOVED TO GO OUT CAMPING
IN TENTS BY THE LAGOON,
HOPING IT WOULD NOT RAIN AS THEY
SLEPT UNDER THE MOON...

THE PROBLEM WAS THAT SOMETIMES
HIS FRIENDS WOULD FIND IT FRIGHTENING.
FOR SOMETIMES WHEN HE BOTTOM-BURPED
IT WAS LIKE THUNDER AND LIGHTNING!

THEY ALSO LIKED THE LIBRARY,
WHERE THEY LOVED TO SIT AND READ,
IN SILENT PEACE AND QUIET,
WITH ALL THE BOOKS THEY'D EVER NEED...

FICTION→

←NON-FICTION

THE PROBLEM WAS THAT SOMETIMES
HIS FRIENDS GOT QUITE A SCARE.
FOR SOMETIMES WHEN HE BOTTOM-BURPED
IT SOUNDED LIKE A BEAR!

THEY ALSO LOVED TO SWIM TOGETHER,
SPLASHING IN THE POOL,
PLAYING IN THE SUNSHINE
WITH THE WATER TO KEEP COOL...

THE PROBLEM WAS THAT SOMETIMES
HIS FRIENDS HID INSIDE THE CAVE,
FOR SOMETIMES WHEN HE BOTTOM-BURPED
IT CAUSED A TIDAL WAVE!

ANOTHER THING THEY LOVED TO PLAY
WAS THE MUSICAL STATUES GAME,
WHERE STILLNESS WHEN THE MUSIC STOPS
WAS EVERYBODY'S AIM...

THE PROBLEM WAS THAT SOMETIMES
HIS FRIENDS SAID THE GROUND WOULD SHAKE.
FOR SOMETIMES WHEN HE BOTTOM-BURPED
IT CAUSED A SMALL EARTHQUAKE!

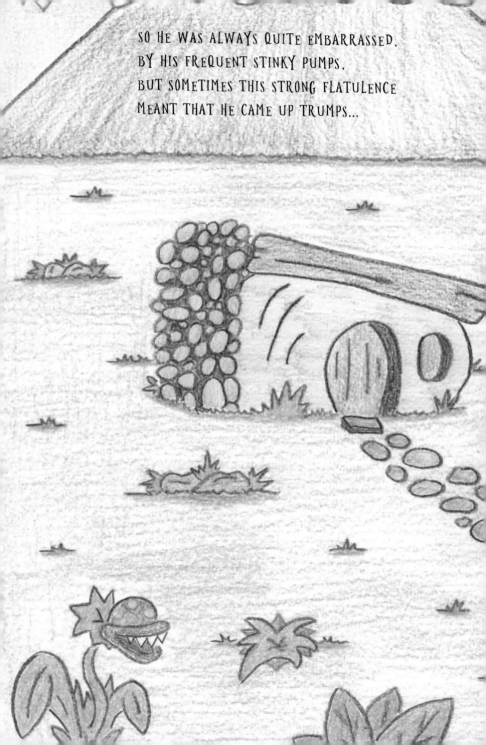

SO HE WAS ALWAYS QUITE EMBARRASSED,
BY HIS FREQUENT STINKY PUMPS.
BUT SOMETIMES THIS STRONG FLATULENCE
MEANT THAT HE CAME UP TRUMPS...

ONE DAY A BIG BAD WOLF CAME
AND HE CREPT AROUND THE TOWN,
STEALING LOTS OF FOOD
AND BLOWING LOTS OF HOUSES DOWN.

BUT PUMPOSAURUS WASN'T SCARED,
HE'D HAD ABOUT ENOUGH.
HE HID AND WAITED FOR THE WOLF
TO START TO HUFF AND PUFF...

RIGHT THEN HE DID WHAT HE DID BEST,
I'M RATHER PLEASED TO SAY.
HE DID A MASSIVE BOTTOM-BURP
AND BLEW THE WOLF AWAY!

THE WHOLE TOWN WAS DELIGHTED
AND HIS FRIENDS WERE VERY PROUD,
IT DIDN'T MATTER THAT HIS BOTTOM-BURPS
WERE VERY LOUD...

OR THAT THE SMELL HE CONJURED UP
INSIDE HIS LITTLE BELLY,
MADE THE AIR AROUND HIM
TASTE LIKE CARPET-FLAVOURED JELLY!

SO I'M PLEASED TO SAY THAT HERE WE HAVE A HAPPY EVER AFTER.
WHERE EVERYONE (EXCEPT THE WOLF) COULD LIVE WITH JOY AND LAUGHTER...

BECAUSE OF ONE BRAVE DINOSAUR,
WHOSE BOTTOM BURPED A CHORUS.
HE REALLY WAS A HERO
AND HIS NAME WAS PUMPOSAURUS!